Jackson and Julia, a daring pair
Boarded a plane, without a care
Their parents and experts, by their side
Adventure awaited, they couldn't hide

The engines roared, the wheels took flight
They soared over mountains, an amazing sight
The jungle awaited, down below
With creatures and dangers, they didn't know

The plane touched down, the adventure began
They met their guides, with a wave and a hand
They set up camp, in the heart of the land
Excitement building, they had a plan

To explore and discover, the wonders within
The beauty and danger, they'd have to win
With courage and bravery, they'd push
through the night
And come out the other side, with a treasure
in sight

The plane had landed, and they'd arrived
To the jungle, where they would thrive
The trees towered high, the vines hung low
A place so mysterious, they'd yet to know

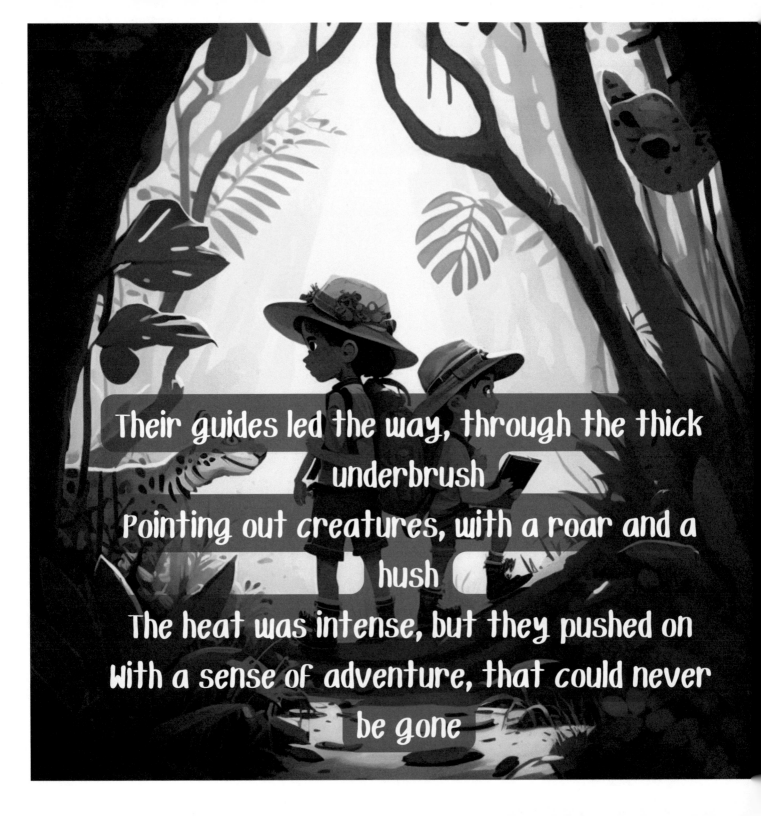

Their guides led the way, through the thick underbrush
Pointing out creatures, with a roar and a hush
The heat was intense, but they pushed on
With a sense of adventure, that could never be gone

They arrived at camp, a place to call home
To rest and to eat, and to write in their tomes
The fire was lit, and the stars shone bright
As they shared stories, of the day and the night

The jungle was alive, with sounds all around
From chirping birds, to the roar of the ground
They knew they were in for an adventure so true
A journey so grand, with wonders anew.

The jungle was alive, with creatures galore
Jackson and Julia, were eager for more
The guides set traps, to catch the unknown
To learn and discover, how the creatures had grown

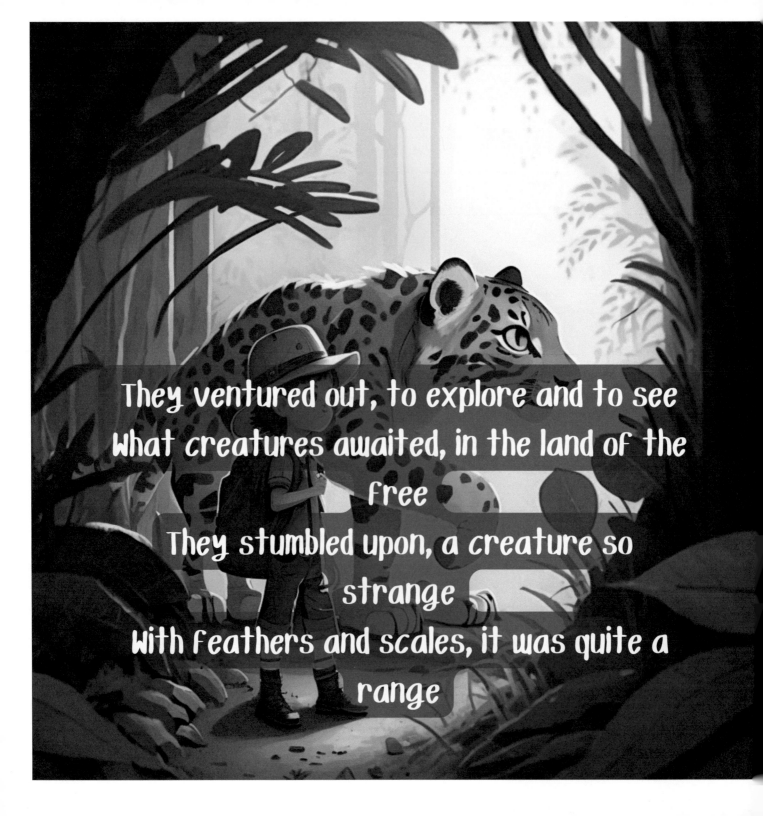

They ventured out, to explore and to see
What creatures awaited, in the land of the free
They stumbled upon, a creature so strange
With feathers and scales, it was quite a range

The creature stared, with a curious eye
As they captured it, with a skillful tie
They studied and learned, the creature's ways
And released it back, to the jungle's maze

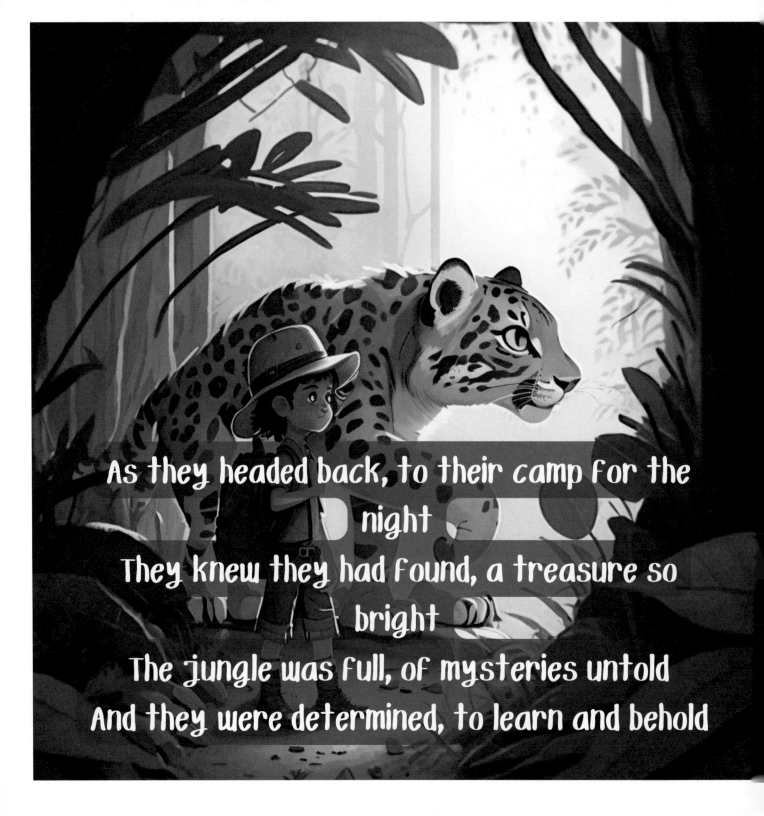

As they headed back, to their camp for the night
They knew they had found, a treasure so bright
The jungle was full, of mysteries untold
And they were determined, to learn and behold

Chapter 4: The Search for the Lost Temple

The map they had found, was their guide
To a lost temple, they'd never before spied
Jackson and Julia, with their guides so true
Set out on a journey, with a treasure in view

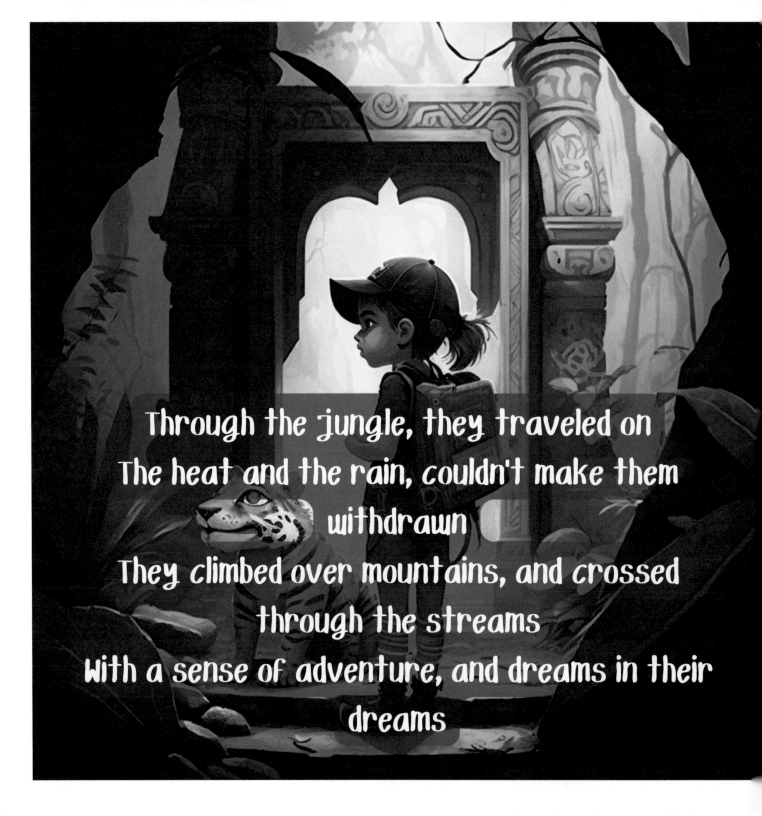

Through the jungle, they traveled on
The heat and the rain, couldn't make them withdrawn
They climbed over mountains, and crossed through the streams
With a sense of adventure, and dreams in their dreams

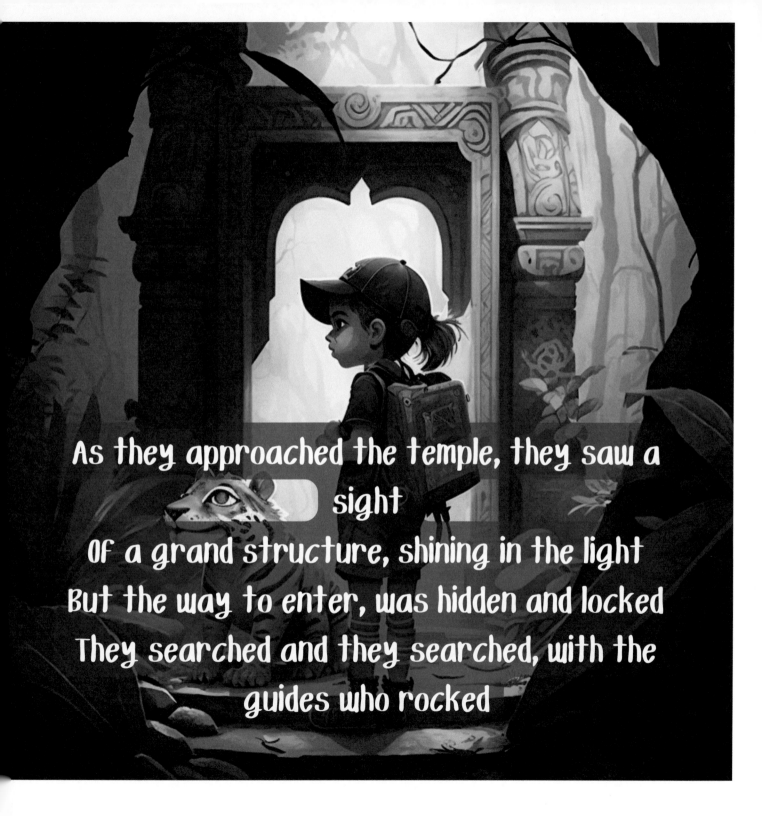

As they approached the temple, they saw a sight
Of a grand structure, shining in the light
But the way to enter, was hidden and locked
They searched and they searched, with the guides who rocked

Then they found, a hidden door
A passage so dark, they couldn't see anymore
They entered the temple, with their torches bright
And found the treasure, that was their delight

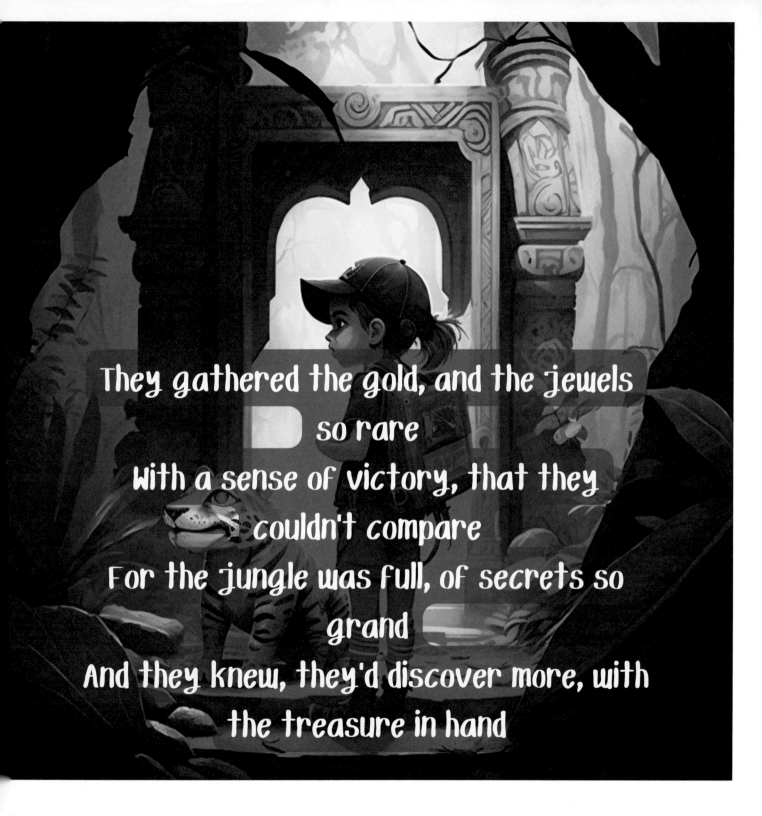

They gathered the gold, and the jewels
so rare
With a sense of victory, that they
couldn't compare
For the jungle was full, of secrets so
grand
And they knew, they'd discover more, with
the treasure in hand

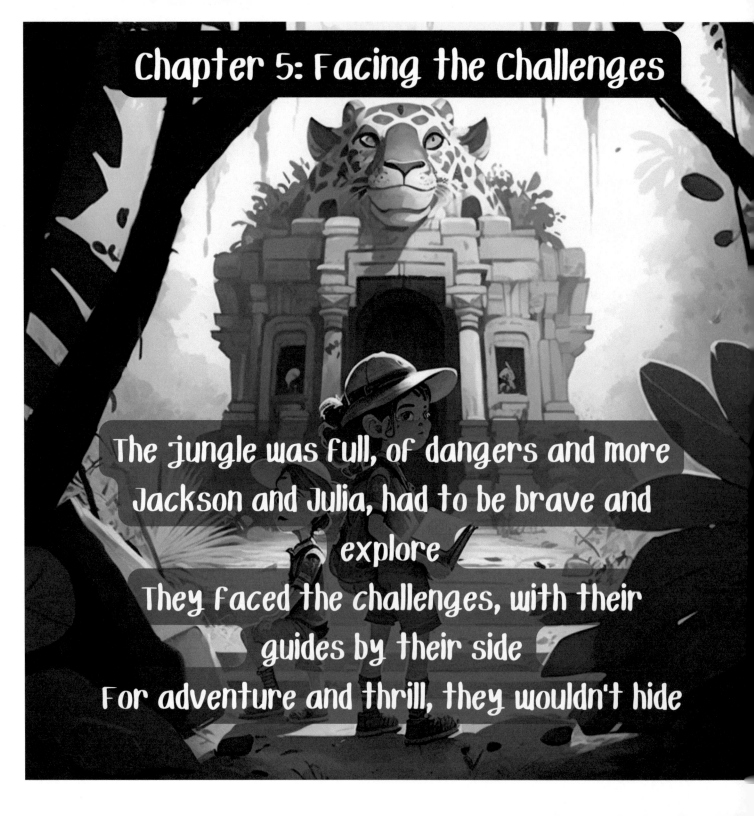

Chapter 5: Facing the Challenges

The jungle was full, of dangers and more
Jackson and Julia, had to be brave and
explore
They faced the challenges, with their
guides by their side
For adventure and thrill, they wouldn't hide

The river was deep, and the current so strong
They had to cross it, to journey along
With ropes and with skills, they made their way through
Their strength and their courage, never askew

Then, they came across, a creature so rare
A giant snake, with a deadly glare
They had to be smart, to avoid its strike
For their safety and survival, were not to be like

As they pushed forward, through the heat and the rain
They knew that their efforts, wouldn't be in vain
For the jungle was full, of wonders and awe
And they were determined, to discover it all.

Chapter 6: Making New Friends

The jungle was full, of life and of fun
And Jackson and Julia, were not the only ones
They met a friendly tribe, with a smile and a wave
And welcomed them with open arms, to the tribe's cave

The tribe shared their culture, their food and their dance
And showed them the jungle, with a new glance
They learned of the creatures, and the plants so rare
And discovered the wonders, they couldn't compare

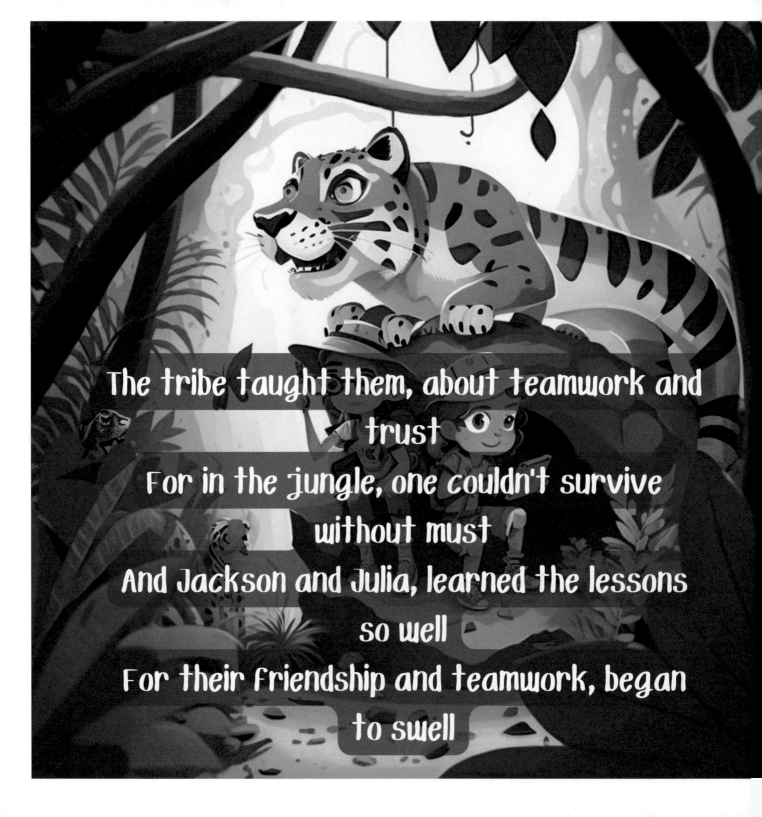

The tribe taught them, about teamwork and trust
For in the jungle, one couldn't survive without must
And Jackson and Julia, learned the lessons so well
For their friendship and teamwork, began to swell

As they said their goodbyes, to the tribe so grand
They knew that their journey, was not to an end
For the jungle was full, of friendship and cheer
And they were grateful, for the memories so dear.

Chapter 7: The Final Stretch

The lost temple, had been found
The treasure, had been unbound
And now, with the journey's end in sight
Jackson and Julia, were filled with delight

The final stretch, was the toughest yet
The heat and the rain, they'd never forget
But with the treasure, in their hands so tight
They pushed on, with all their might

As they reached, the end of the trail
Their hearts, began to exhale
For the journey, had been so grand
And the treasures, were like gold in their
hand

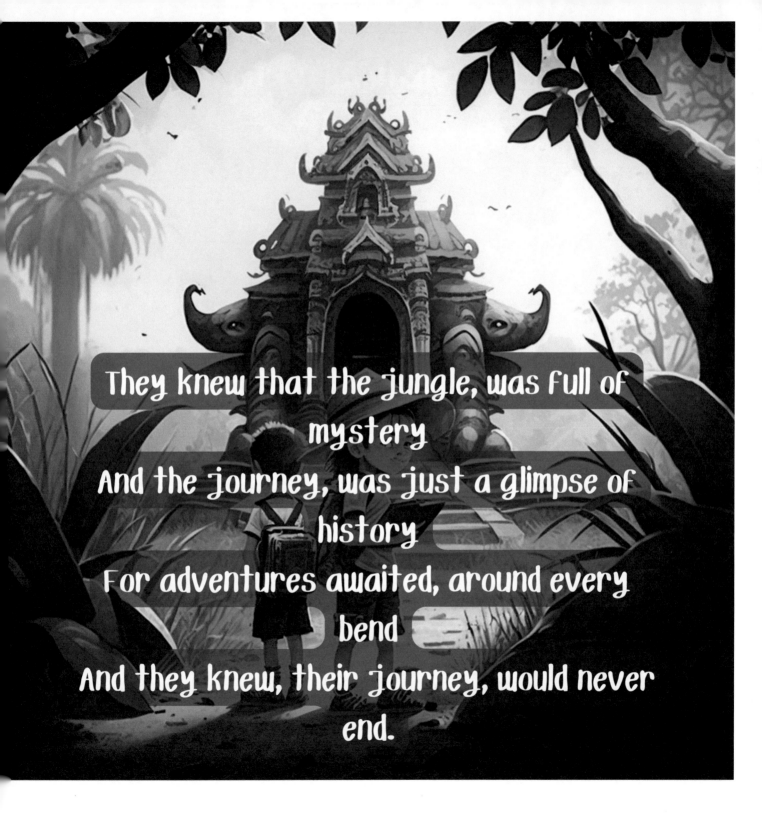

They knew that the jungle, was full of mystery
And the journey, was just a glimpse of history
For adventures awaited, around every bend
And they knew, their journey, would never end.

Chapter 8: Heading Home

The jungle adventure, had come to an end
And Jackson and Julia, were headed home, my friend
They said their goodbyes, to the guides and the tribe
And felt a sense of pride, for their adventure vibe

The plane was waiting, to take them away
And the memories, would be with them, every day
As they soared over the mountains, and the sea
They reflected, on the journey, and how it would be

For the jungle, had taught them, so much to see
The beauty, the danger, and the mystery
And Jackson and Julia, had learned so well
To explore and to dream, and to never quell

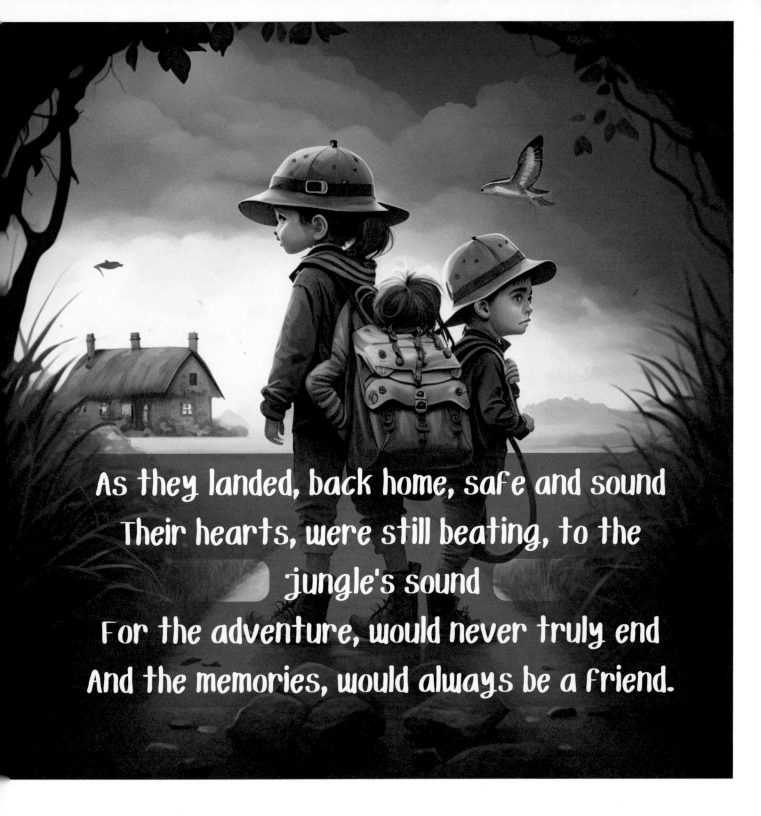

As they landed, back home, safe and sound
Their hearts, were still beating, to the
jungle's sound
For the adventure, would never truly end
And the memories, would always be a friend.

Epilogue: The Adventure Continues

The adventure was over, but the journey was not done

For Jackson and Julia, the jungle had just begun

The memories they'd made, would forever stay

And the lessons they'd learned, would guide them on their way

For the jungle, had taught them, to be brave and true
To explore and to dream, and to always pursue
The wonders of life, that waited out there
And to never give up, no matter how rare

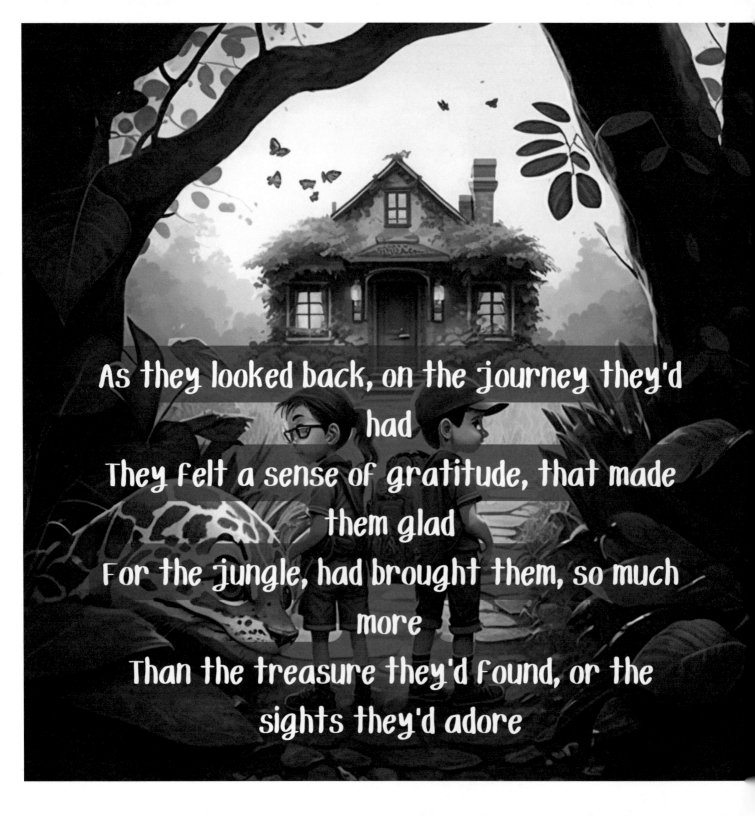

As they looked back, on the journey they'd had
They felt a sense of gratitude, that made them glad
For the jungle, had brought them, so much more
Than the treasure they'd found, or the sights they'd adore

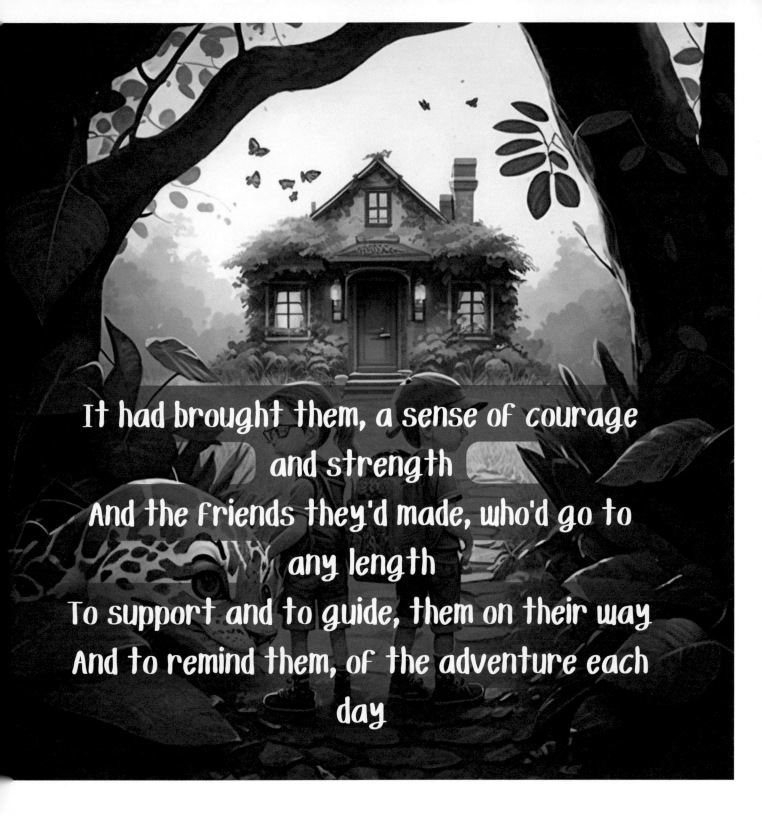

It had brought them, a sense of courage and strength
And the friends they'd made, who'd go to any length
To support and to guide, them on their way
And to remind them, of the adventure each day

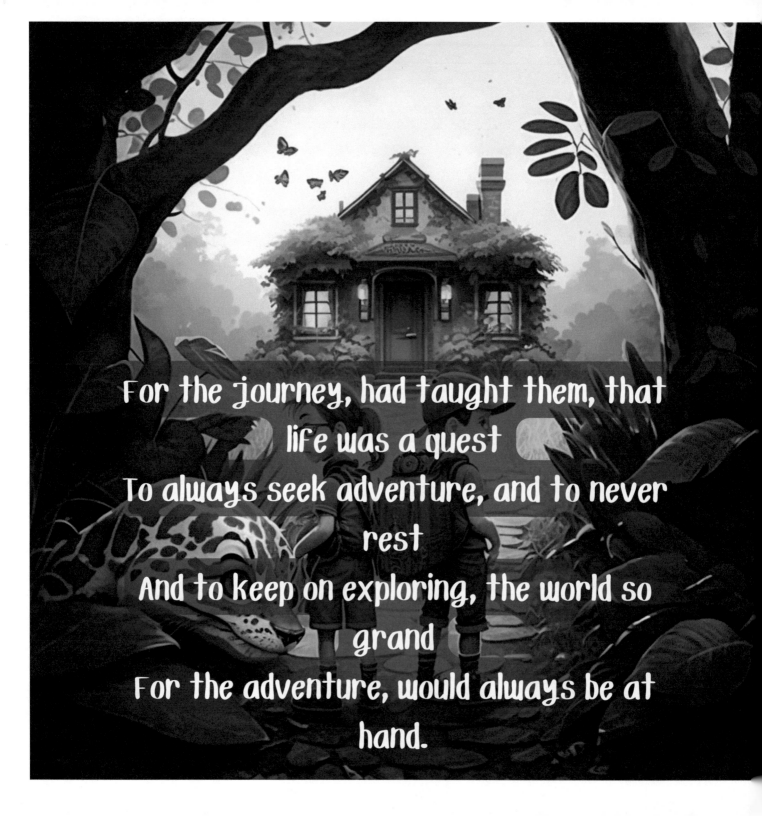

For the journey, had taught them, that life was a quest
To always seek adventure, and to never rest
And to keep on exploring, the world so grand
For the adventure, would always be at hand.

Made in United States
Troutdale, OR
12/17/2023

16145660R00024